"Because I'm A Pit Bull"

Renèe Washington

Illustrated by: Roberto Oquendo

Enjoy!
Renèe Washington

AuthorHouse™
1663 Liberty Drive
Bloomington, IN 47403
www.authorhouse.com
Phone: 1-800-839-8640

First published by AuthorHouse 10/14/2011

ISBN: 978-1-4670-7024-9 (sc)

Library of Congress Control Number: 2011918812

Printed in the United States of America

Any people depicted in stock imagery provided by Thinkstock are models,
and such images are being used for illustrative purposes only.
Certain stock imagery © Thinkstock.

This book is printed on acid-free paper.

authorHOUSE®

This book is dedicated to my pit Bull, Zena.

Everyone expects that I should bite people.

. . . because I'm a Pit Bull

4

The Truth is: I love people, and expect a pet on the head.

. . . but, because I'm a Pit Bull.

Everyone expects that I should chase and harm cats.

. . . because I'm a Pit Bull.

The Truth is: I Like cats, and want to learn more about them.

. . . but, because I'm a pit Bull.

Everyone expects that it's my fault when smaller dogs run toward me, and bark in my face.

. . . because I'm a Pit Bull.

The Truth is: I Really want to get along with smaller dogs, and expect them to be my friend.

. . . but, because I'm a Pit Bull.

Children tease me, and Grown-Ups give me mean stares when I go for a walk.

. . . because I'm a Pit Bull

The Truth is: I Expect kind words and love from children and grown-ups.

. . . but because I'm a Pit Bull.

Everyone expects that I should be fierce, and unafraid when thunder and lightening occurs.

. . . because I'm a Pit Bull.

The Truth is: No One expects that I tremble, shake, and hide under the bed during a thunderstorm.

. . . but, because I'm a Pit Bull.

Everyone expects me to be a fighter, and have lots of puppies to follow in my footsteps.

. . . because I'm a Pit Bull.

The Truth is: I am a pet. My Mommy had me spayed so that I can live a longer, and healthier life.

. . . but, because I'm a Pit Bull.

CPSIA information can be obtained
at www.ICGtesting.com
Printed in the USA
255988LV00002B